## How to use this book

This book is designed to be read initially by children and adults together. It is not an explanation of what cancer is, but a book about the impact the diagnosis of childhood cancer can have on a sibling's life. It is a starting point for discussion, giving the adult a way in to ask about the child's own experience of difficult situations. On each page one of the illustrations has been left for the child to colour in.

First Edition 2005

Second Edition 2010

ISBN 978-0-9551642-4-8

Published by:

**CLAN Cancer Support**
**CLAN House**
120 Westburn Road
Aberdeen
AB25 2QA

Printed by ✕I⊏.com

# MIKKI HAS CANCER

By Eileen Wheeler

&

Illustrated by Iiris Maanoja

CLAN

cancer support for all

Mikki is my little brother. He has blonde hair that sticks up like a hedgehog and green eyes that are a bit like the cat's. He has just had his 6th birthday party and he has cancer.

When I first heard Mikki had cancer I didn't believe it. I thought cancer was something old people got, not children, and not my brother.

The doctor at the hospital told mum and dad about the cancer, and then they told my granny and grandad, nana and I'm not sure who else. I was scared because I hadn't seen adults crying before. So it had to be really serious. They tried to hide their tears from me but I would catch them sometimes.

Mikki had mum to himself all the time in hospital, and he got loads of presents even though it wasn't Christmas or his birthday. Everyone brought presents to the ward or sent parcels to our house for Mikki. He didn't even say thank you for them! Nobody sent me a present and I was trying to be brave and good.

Just after we found
out about the cancer,
mum and Mikki went to the hospital to stay there, so he could start
his treatment. I didn't want Mikki to be alone, but I wanted my mum
at home too. It was lonely without Mikki in the house and a bit scary.
And what if mum was too busy caring for Mikki and forgot about me?

I didn't like it when Mikki
had to stay in hospital to
get his chemotherapy medicine, or
was rushed in to hospital when I was at school.
It was lonely at home, especially at night. I used to climb into his bed
and fall asleep there. I missed Mikki and didn't want him to be ill. I
wanted it to be like before.

Sometimes I didn't know who would collect me from school and I'd be bad-tempered all day. Mum tried to be there, but when Mikki was poorly it was nana or Sam's mum or Liam's mum or Matthew's mum who collected me.

At school the other
children always asked lots of questions or
said stupid things. 'Where's Mikki?' 'Why does
Mikki have a bald head?' 'Is he going to die?' 'Are you going
to get cancer too?' 'You can't play with us, we don't want to catch
cancer'. I know you can't catch cancer, but I wished they would leave
me alone. My teacher, Mrs Ross, was kind to me and each morning
asked me quietly if I was okay. I know I can tell her if I am upset.

When Mikki was at home mum fussed over him. If he said he was hot or had a sore tummy she always listened to him and stopped everything to check his temperature straight away. Sometimes I wanted to shout 'What about me? I'm here too!' Sometimes I pretended I had a sore leg or sore tummy to get mum to check me out too.

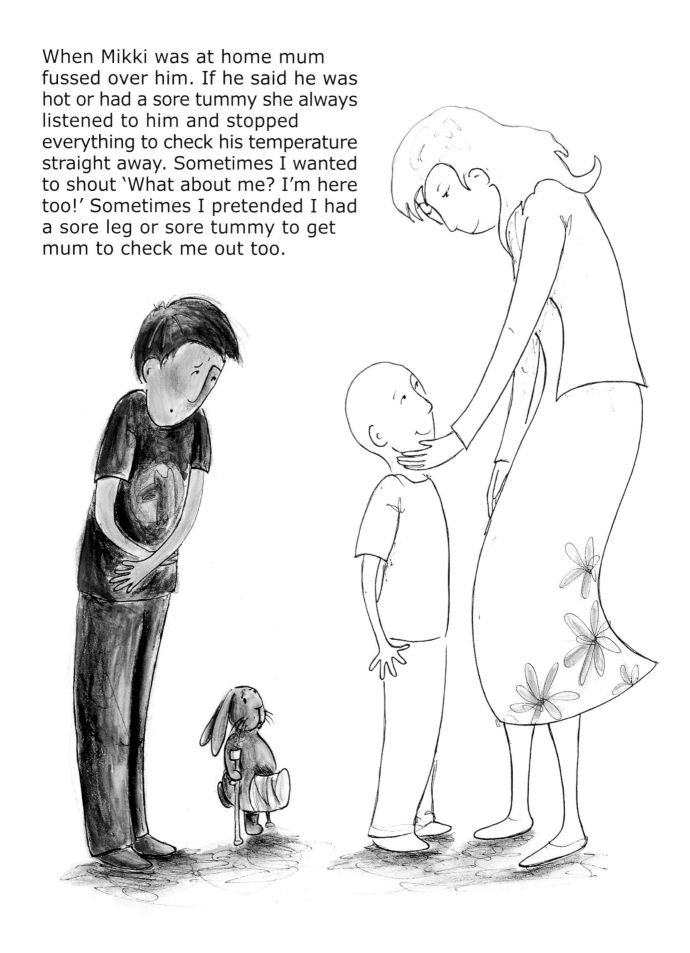

If Mikki didn't eat his dinner mum said it was okay, but I had to eat mine or got into trouble. When Mikki was taking some of his medicine he was horrible to mum and he didn't get into trouble for giving her cheek. I always do. That's not fair. Mum says it's the medicine being horrid, not Mikki, but I'm not sure.

I like it when I can play in the garden with Mikki, at chasing or pretend fighting. It is like it was before he was ill, but then Mikki will say 'Don't hit me, I've got cancer. I'll tell mum on you.' That makes me angry because he still hits me as hard as he can.

I am looking forward to Mikki just being Mikki again, without his wiggly, his feeding tube, with hair that stays in and not having to go to the hospital all the time, that won't happen for a while but I hope it will not be too long. Then we can have proper pretend fights and chases, I will teach him to swim and we can do other things we are missing out on at the moment.

Eileen Wheeler is the support worker for children and young people with CLAN, a cancer support charity. Her role is to support any child or young person affected by cancer, whether as a patient, relative or friend. She can provide information at a level suited to the individual, and allow the child to explore his/her feelings in a safe and secure environment. Support can be offered on an individual basis or in groups. Eileen is a qualified social worker, who previously worked at the Royal Aberdeen Children's Hospital where she supported families who had a child diagnosed with cancer.

CLAN is a registered charity which has been operating in North East Scotland, Orkney and Shetland since 1983. It provides support and information to anyone affected by cancer.